DISNEP
MICKEY
&FRIENDS

GET READY
for SCHOOL

 PRESS

Los Angeles • New York

First Hardcover Edition, July 2020
10 9 8 7 6 5 4 3 2 1
ISBN 978-1-368-04835-4
FAC-038091-20143
Printed in the United States of America
Visit www.disneybooks.com

CONTENTS

• • • • • • •

SUPER SCHOOL DAY

Written by LAUREN CLAUSS

Illustrated by the DISNEY STORYBOOK ART TEAM

HUEY, DEWEY, AND LOUIE

were so excited. The first day of school was coming up! They couldn't wait to visit their uncle Donald. He had promised to help them get ready.

When they arrived, Mickey, Minnie, and Goofy were already there. The whole gang was going to help!

"Are you boys ready for the first day?" Mickey asked.

"Do you have your backpacks packed?" Minnie added.

"We're not ready at all!" Dewey told them.
"We don't even know what we *should* have!"
Huey said.

Goofy, Donald, and Mickey exchanged
nervous looks as the nephews ran off to
gather supplies.

"Is this what we're supposed to bring?" Louie asked after grabbing everything he thought they'd need . . . including camping gear.

Donald couldn't believe it. "Boys, we've got a lot of work to do."

"Let's start with my favorite school supply,"
Mickey said. "Snacks!"

Mickey and the gang took Donald's nephews
to the grocery store and picked out some
healthy snacks.

Donald, Goofy, Daisy, and Minnie gathered even more school supplies for Huey, Dewey, and Louie at the store.

"Gawrsh, I wish it was *my* first day of school again," Goofy said.

"Me too!" Daisy chimed in.

When Donald's nephews and the gang got home, it was time to pack their backpacks.

"More stickers in my backpack, please!" Huey shouted.

"Can I have some apple slices, Minnie?" Dewey asked.

"Don't forget the glue sticks . . . oh, and the tissues . . . and my new pencils!"

Louie cheered.

The next morning, the nephews got up bright and early for their first day of school. Their backpacks were stuffed, their snacks were packed, and Huey, Dewey, and Louie were excited about what the day would bring.

When they got to school, they couldn't wait to go inside. They had a new teacher to meet, new friends to make, and new things to learn.

The nephews introduced themselves to the other students and their teacher.

"I'm Huey!"

"And I'm Dewey!"

"My name's Louie!"

After everyone else said hello, they found their seats and started the first lesson of the day.

Later on, after lunch and math, it was time
for Huey's favorite class of the day . . . art!
Huey painted something red—the color of
his shirt. "School is so fun!" he said.
"Totally!" his brothers agreed.

Next was Dewey's favorite class—language arts! He really liked learning, and his teacher was nice.

After school, they took the school bus back to
Uncle Donald's house.

"I can't wait to tell Uncle Donald all about our day!"
Dewey said.

"It was all so fun I can't even pick a favorite class!"
Louie said.

"Uncle Donald! Uncle Donald!" they cheered as they ran through the door. "We're ready for our *second* day of school!"

But Donald was asleep. It's hard work getting three kids ready for school!

HUEY, DEWEY, and LOUIE'S RAINY DAY

Written by **KATE RITCHEY**

Illustrated by the **DISNEY STORYBOOK ART TEAM**

and **LOTER, INC.**

THE BOYS LOVED to visit their uncle. He had a big backyard and lots of toys to play with. But their favorite part of visiting was playing with Donald.

Huey rang the doorbell.

"Hiya, Uncle Donald!" they shouted when he opened the door.

"Oh, hello, boys," said Donald. "I was just getting ready to read the newspaper."

Huey and Dewey pushed past Donald.
"Did you get any new toys?" asked Huey.
"What kind of snacks do you have?"
asked Dewey.

Louie grabbed his uncle's arm. "Come play
with us, Uncle Donald," he said.
But Donald just wanted to read his paper.

"Let's go play in the backyard!" Huey said.
He swung open the back door. Suddenly . . .

CRASH! BOOM!

Lightning flashed in the windows.
Thunder rumbled through the house.

"Oh, no!" the boys cried. "We cannot go outside now! What are we going to do?"

"We could play a game," Dewey said. "I will be blue!"

"I am red!" said Huey.

"I will be green!" said Louie. "You can be yellow, Uncle Donald."

The boys played three games. Dewey won
every time.

Donald was *not* having fun!

"Maybe we should do something else,"
said Huey.

"How about painting?" he said. He found paint
and paintbrushes in the closet.

"You can hang our pictures on the wall,"
Louie told Donald.

Donald thought painting was too messy.
"Why don't you boys have some hot chocolate?" he said.
"I am going to read the newspaper."

The boys watched the rain and listened to the thunder.

"There must be something fun we can do," said Huey.

The boys looked at Donald. He had fallen asleep
in his chair.

"I have a great idea!" Dewey said. "Let's build
a fort."

The brothers gathered sheets, towels, blankets, and pillows. They took cushions from the couch and chairs from the kitchen.

Soon construction began on the fort!

Huey built a lookout tower to spy on anyone outside the fort.

Dewey built a secret entrance. The boys had to crawl under two chairs and over a footstool to get inside!

Louie was in charge of supplies. He piled up
everything the boys would need.

Donald was still sleeping. He did not know
that the boys were building around him.

At last, Fort McDuck was complete!
The main room of the fort was big, with
lots of space to camp out. The lookout
let the boys watch for invaders.

Fort McDuck

The fort's kitchen had all kinds of snacks.
And the secret entrance was so well hidden
no one would ever find it!

Suddenly, thunder boomed through the fort's walls.
"We are being attacked!" yelled Huey.

Huey, Dewey, and Louie bravely defended
Fort McDuck.
"Hooray!" they yelled. "The fort is safe!"

All the cheering woke up Donald. He opened his eyes to find that he was surrounded by pillows and sheets.

"What is going on?" he asked.

"Do not worry, Uncle Donald," said Louie.
"We saved you from the invaders attacking
Fort McDuck!" Dewey added.

"Hey!" said Huey from the lookout. "The rain has stopped."

"Now can we go play outside?" Dewey asked Donald.

"I think that is a great idea!" said Donald.

The boys crawled out of the fort. They put on their rain boots and coats. Donald stayed inside the fort, where it was quiet. He could finish reading his newspaper.

"Hooray!" shouted Huey, Dewey, and Louie as they jumped into the rain puddles. It was the perfect ending to their day at Uncle Donald's house!

A SUMMER DAY

Adapted from *Donald Takes a Trip,* by **KATE RITCHEY**

Illustrated by the **DISNEY STORYBOOK ART TEAM**

IT WAS A HOT SUMMER DAY.

Mickey Mouse and his friends were relaxing in his living room. The friends were just deciding what to do with their day when *pop!* Mickey's air-conditioning broke!

"Maybe there will be a breeze outside," said Minnie. But there was no breeze, just nice cool lemonade from Mickey's refrigerator.

"What are we going to do now?"
asked Daisy.

Minnie looked around. "Hmmm . . ."
she said. "Maybe we could make fans.
Or we could try sitting in the shade
under the tree. . . ."

"Gosh! Those sprinklers look nice and cool!" said Goofy, pointing down at Mickey's lawn.

Donald nodded. "But there isn't enough water coming out of them to keep us cool!" he said.

As Minnie watched her friends looking at the sprinklers, she suddenly had an idea.

Minnie jumped out of her chair. "I've got it!" she shouted.
"Let's go to the lake! There's always a breeze there, and
there's so much to do!"

"What a great idea!" said Mickey.

"It is the perfect day for a swim," Daisy added.

Minnie and her friends raced home to pack. Minnie quickly threw her bathing suit and a towel into her bag. Then she headed back to Mickey's house.

In no time, the friends were on their way. They were so excited for their day at the lake!

"What should we do first?" Minnie asked.

Everyone had a different idea. Daisy wanted to play basketball. Mickey and Pluto wanted to play fetch. And Donald wanted to go fishing!

Before anyone could stop him, Donald
raced off toward a little boat docked
beside the water.

Donald was about to hop into the boat when Minnie called out to him. "Wait up, Donald," she said. "I don't think we can all fit in the boat. Let's do something together!"

"But the water looks so nice!" said Donald.

"Why don't we go for a swim?" said Minnie. "We can all do that!"

Donald finally agreed. After all, they had come to the lake to go swimming.

The friends put away their toys and jumped into the water. . . .

"Aah," said Donald. "You were right, Minnie. This *was* a good idea!"

Minnie smiled to herself. She was glad she and her friends had found a way to cool off.

"I could stay in this water all day!" Daisy said.
And that was just what they did.

As the sun set and the day started to get cooler,
Minnie and her friends got out of the water.
Minnie had one last surprise for her friends . . . s'mores!

"Gee, Minnie," said Mickey as they roasted marshmallows over a campfire, "you really do know how to plan the perfect day!"

Finally, it really was time to leave. Minnie and her friends packed their bags and got into the car.

"That was so much fun!" said Donald as they drove home. "Let's do it again tomorrow!"

HOW I SPENT
MY SUMMER VACATION

• • • • • • • •

What did you do all summer?
On a separate piece of paper, draw your
favorite summer activity or what you
did on your summer vacation.
Do you have a story you might want to
tell on the first day of school?
Maybe it goes with your drawing.
Think about it and practice telling it
so you're ready to do it for
your class!

How I Spent
My Summer Vacation
By Mickey Mouse

Hiya, everybody!
Wanna hear how I spent my summer vacation?
Well, all right! Donald wanted to go hiking,
and Daisy wanted to go sightseeing.
I wanted to go to the beach.
Minnie and Goofy liked that idea because
Minnie wanted to surf and
Goofy wanted to collect seashells.
So we headed for the beach!

We had fun splashing in the waves and building
sandcastles. Donald got to hike in the sand dunes,
and Daisy took a little sightseeing trip on a boat.
We even went snorkeling and saw all kinds
of fish and sea creatures.
At night we made a campfire and
roasted marshmallows.
Gosh! It was swell!

TIPS FOR PARENTS

• • • • • • • •

AS SUMMER COMES TO AN END, help yourself and your kids by preparing physically, mentally, and emotionally for going back to school. Here are some tips you can use to set up routines, get organized, and plan ahead. Make sure to include your kids in as many decisions as possible so they're on board and cooperative! Happy school days to you!

1 Get kids' **sleep schedules** back to school bedtimes two weeks before the first day of school.

2 Before school starts, **visit museums and cultural attractions** to get them back in the habit of thinking and questioning.

3 **Read with your kids** all summer before school starts, or if they're old enough, get them to read on their own. You can create a reading log for them and/or join a summer library reading program.

4 Try out different **homework apps** that will help organize your kids' homework assignments.

5 Have **weekly home meetings** to review schedules for the coming week.

6 Go over **rules** about "screen time" for during the school year and on weekdays in particular.

7 Establish a set **family time**, whether it's breakfast, dinner, or before bed, where the focus is on the kids.

8 **Discuss what kids can expect** on the first day of school so they feel prepared.

9 **Get lists ahead of time** of school supplies, books, and technology that your kids will need.

10 **Include your kids** on shopping trips for back-to-school supplies and let them choose some of their own items.

11 Create a **dedicated space** for organizing school supplies and doing homework.

12 Help your kids **develop a system** for organizing homework assignments and class documents.

13 Set up **regular trips to the library** during the school year for activities and/or just reading.

14 Create a **family calendar** that tracks everyone's classroom and after-school activities and commitments.

15 Create an **after-school schedule** allowing for snacks, relaxation, play, study, and chores.

16 Create and discuss a **morning routine** *before* school starts.

17 Clean out kids' rooms (by **decluttering**) and get clothes ready.

18 Shop for and **prepare ahead** for school lunches and snacks.

19 **Plan ahead** for what commitments you're willing to make during school—chaperoning field trips, being a classroom parent, etc.

20 **Talk openly** with your kids about their feelings about going back to school.